T0103526

STATEMENT

Statement participates is Prestigious International Book Fairs such as:

Frankfurt Book Fair

As the biggest book and media fair in the world, it has attracted roughly 7,500 exhibitors from over 100 countries. As the whole industry gathers, business opportunities and networking activities are endless.

London Book Fair

This fair is considered a global marketplace for negotiating sales, distribution, and content rights across different platforms, having over 24,000 attendees from 124 countries in 2014 alone.

BookExpo America

This event offers a dynamic environment for sourcing new titles, building relationships, and discovering the latest technology trends as well as educational programs to support your success.

Guadalajara Book Fair

This fair is focused on professionals and the public alike. Over nine days, Guadalajara is transformed into the epitome of the book industry, as book enthusiasts congregate to experience one of the most renowned international literary festivals.

Beijing International Book Fair

In the past 20 years, this fair has become a prominent feature in the publishing industry. In 2013, it boasted over 2,000 exhibitors from 76 countries, incorporating copyright trade, book trade, cultural events, displays, consultation services, and professional networking.

Miami Book Fair International 2016 Book Gallery

Each year, the Miami Book Fair International brings together hundreds of thousands of book lovers to celebrate the written word.

STATEMENT

Kavya Khemka

PARTRIDGE

Cover Designed by: Pixamatic Communications Pvt. Ltd.

ISBN:	Hardcover	978-1-4828-8466-1
	Softcover	978-1-4828-8479-1
	eBook	978-1-4828-8465-4

Print information available on the last page.

To order additional copies of this book, contact
Partridge India
000 800 10062 62
orders.india@partridgepublishing.com

www.partridgepublishing.com/india

AUTHOR'S NOTE

As a writer, I have made my first attempt at book writing. Since the tender age of three, I started reading but never thought that one day I would attempt to write my own book. I am sure that I have done a great job, but I hope my effort is also appreciated by my readers. As it's my first book, it has been the most incredible experience for me.

I would like to thank Sonia Aunty (Mrs Sonia Rajore), my mentor in creative writing, for her helpful and encouraging guidance. I owe all my vocabulary and grammar to her and her blessings. As a child, I had written many stories—some big, some small (which every child does), but it was only Sonia Aunty who found the author in me and pushed me into book writing. Ma'am, a big hug from me to you, thank you for being always there. I owe it all to you.

This would not have been possible without my mom. She encouraged me to read and write stories at a nascent stage in life and also assisted me in pursuing my dream. The critic in her made me aware of my potential. Mom, I know I have given you sleepless nights at the time of deciding my script, but you have always been very cooperative, helpful, and patient with me. Love you, mom, for everything.

Not to forget my Dad (Daddy) who, at every step, told me that he is very proud of me, which helped me to want to give my best.

Book writing requires calmness and patience in the mind, which I achieved with the help, support, and encouragement from Nooreen Teacher (Ms Nooreen Madhani). Thank you for everything. Without you, my book would have taken off but never crossed the difficult roads the way it has.

Another very important person I would like to thank is my Nanu (Nanaji or Mr Ashok Lohia) for teaching me how to utilise my time constructively and how to make the most of my inborn and acquired skills. Nanu, all I can say is that I know you will always be there for me, and that means the world to me. I am grateful, Nanu, for all your timely advice and examples.

My English teacher, Sadhvi, ma'am, thank you for always being there when I have a problem and for improving my language.

I have enjoyed every bit of creating my first book right from deciding the script, putting it in words, and all the steps it required of help, guidance, encouragement, editing, etc.

As a matter of fact, my undying love and passion for books and the constant adventure into fantasy of print land has helped me achieve the desire to write a book. Thus, as an author now, I would recommend and request every single child to start reading at an early age.

Thank you.

Happy reading!

My elder cousin

Riya Didi

Miss you!

CHAPTER 1

One evening during supper, our entire family was gorging on wholesome hot chicken soup, as that was all we could afford. Every spoon of nourishment was being relished as there was always an uncertainty about the next meal. And to add to the physical agony of my hunger pangs was the mental disturbance aroused from the prominent plaster, which was giving away from the ceiling as the house was really ancient, and the dull dreary look of my cottage was an outcome of an aggressive winter. The storm was fierce and could anytime blow away my cottage. The snow accumulated on the ceiling but could make the house collapse anytime. The walls were thin enough to hear the sound of the galloping of the horses in the distance, which sent fearful vibes through my father's eyes. He looked petrified, and there was sudden silence on the table. The paltry food didn't seem edible anymore. With bated breath, we paused, waiting for the arrival of

King Humaca's messengers, who were quite punctual indeed. There was a sudden eerie silence in the atmosphere as any message from the palace was a challenge in itself. My inquisitiveness led me to the window to have a quick glimpse of the galloping cavalcade. But mother quickly reprimanded from the rear and empathetically commanded, 'Riya, come back and shut the window. We have to go to hear the warning!'

The sound of the bugles had always excited me as I related it to festivity and happiness, but this one was a forewarning from the king, followed by a message which only spread fear. A little sneak peak from the crevice of the window, I could see a messenger wearing shiny red robes with a larger-than-life hat and strong, sturdy, curvy boots. He seemed quite impressive when he jerked open the fabric scroll and read with a baritone.

'A message from King Humaca for all you town members.'

'Mission Instatusquo
Thirty-one people
From our town
Will be randomly selected

By our honorable king.
To visit this town
And a palace in it
Called
Palace of Statement,
The people
Will have to jeopardize
Their lives
To find a hidden statement
With the fear
Of one person dying
Every hour.
For this big risk,
The contestants and their families,
Will get a lifetime
Of free precious water supply.'

With a scowl, he rolled back the scroll and added, 'So it will be tomorrow—thirty-one random selections. Dedication, hardwork, and nimbleness are the keys to this assignment, so get set for the challenge, and I shall meet you tomorrow—same time, same place.' The chariot turned back and galloped away, leaving behind a smoke of dust and uncertainty.

CHAPTER 2

There was a sense of gloom all through the town. Skepticism prevailed largely, and groups of people huddled together in nooks and corners discussing their fate and destiny. Somehow, I didn't feel the same. A sense of elation rose within me with the thought that my family would enjoy a life time supply of water if I was to be chosen as a candidate, since water in Incognito was scarce and procuring it was a herculean task. The Incognitians had to walk long distances for their basic liquid requirements as the earth was barren, and it refused to concede to demands of the poor. Only the monarchy had access, and 2090 would go down into the realms of history as the year of 'nobility', as thirty-one people could avail lifelong water during this water starved era.

There was a mutual sense of fear, as my father and I harbored, that of a loss life and the skepticism whether it was really worth it.

The hollow cavities of my father's eyes spoke volumes about his state of being, and the shiver through my body escalated just looking at him. The denominator of our equation was common, 'Whose names would be spelt out?' The entire day seemed long drawn, and the clocks looked frozen. Every minute was like an hour.

At sunset, the houses were unoccupied as the entire town was pouring with people waiting in anticipation, awaiting king's chariot. And soon, the time arrived. Clouds of dust smoke, galloping horses, and frenzy of emotions simultaneously occurred. The scroll opened, and the hearts missed a beat. The gruffness of the voice created a stir, and he bellowed.

'Are you ready?'

There was a feeble retaliation. 'Yes.'

And he continued to read.

'Rollno. 1 -KensiaWrill
Rollno. 2 - Lonta Ambrace
Rollno. 3- Sminka Flear
Rollno. 4 - MamothimoSwiss
Roll no.5 - Lomus Freelter
Roll no.6 – Tonthany Brusoe

Roll no.7 - Bratty Phoes
Roll no.8 - Fonsenca Ambrace
Roll no 9 - Facancia Flear
Roll no 10 - Trithpill Some
Roll no 11- Tencia Comb
Roll no 12 - Lenrica Spear
Roll no 13- Trientica Toader
Roll no 14 - RiyaMathew (ME)'

My father was inconsolable. His noticeable tears were uncontrollable. He hugged me tight, and in muffled tones, he said, 'Darling, we all know you mean good but not at the cost of losing you.' He wouldn't let go of me, tightening his arm further, when I reassured him, 'I shall be fine and have always been a fighter. Believe me, Dad, I shall see the end of it and come back to you.'

By then, the list announcement was over, and all the participants were asked to step forward. My family held on to me, and it took a lot of convincing from me to move on. And slowly, I moved towards my death knell.

CHAPTER 3

My body felt numb, and it moved lifelessly. I could fathom nothing. I wondered about the purpose why I was getting into this—was it really worth it? And again, another thought struck, 'Water was the least I could give them.' Amidst this mental confusion, I heard my father's concerned voice, 'I volunteer for Riya Mathew.' My reflexes were not working, and I didn't respond to his vocal decision and neither did anyone else. And then he shouted with conviction, 'I said I volunteer for Riya Mathew. 'And the charioteer responded rather vehemently, 'This is the king's final list, and we do not alter decisions.' Everyone dispersed, and the town suddenly seemed to wear a ghostly look.

That night, probably every house in Incognito was immersed with melancholic emotions. The roads were isolated, and eerily, one could not even hear the monotonous sounds of the crickets and the bats. Children were cooped up in their houses, and the pleasant aroma of food in the air was also missing. The stillness of the atmosphere would even put mountains to shame.

Next morning, the gates of the royal palace opened, and his highness welcomed all the participants personally. He said, 'My courageous young men and women of Incognito, I am proud of you all. The Palace of Statements beckons you, and I wish you all the very best.' The king then paraded, had a closer look at all the contestants, and smiled, the feeling of calmness passing by him as he was content with the choice. He ordered the ministers for the badges to be pinned up to the players. My badge was number fourteen, and it instantly lit me up because mom has her birthday on the fourteenth, and the number could prove to be lucky. I guess I was just pacifying myself. The king again walked around and chose number four, Mamothimo Swiss, a man probably in his sixties, as our leader. He was well built, fit, and smart, with salt and pepper hair but sharp and shrewd eyes. A quick analysis concluded in my mind that he had won that position because of his seniority and experience. Mamothimo walked up with great pride, and when asked about his comfort, he replied to the king with whole lot of confidence, 'Your command is my duty. I will take charge and serve my best. How can I refuse your gentle request?' And the king himself pinned up the 'LEADER' badge on his puffed up, high-held chest.

CHAPTER 4

After a few minutes, we left for the airport, and as we were entering, the 'Operation Insatusquo Team' handed us a bag. Each of us got one, and we noticed all of the bags had different colours with our initials sown on the bag beautifully. Mine was a blood red. Everything we received from the palace somewhere gave the feeling of the challenge having begun and sent off some different and vague kind of shivers down my body. But that wasn't yet! Not so soon.

I opened my suspense filled cloth holder to check the contents. I found a beautiful blue bag with stones embellished with lovely beads. I just couldn't resist opening it and seeing what was there inside it. There were three things. The first one was a written obituary, which proclaimed about each one's death, as they wanted us prepared for death and witnessing one fatality every hour. It was kept inside a big green-coloured pouch. The second was an orange box with a tiny book in it, which was all about what one family would get after the death of their family member. The third mailer was in another pink bag. I opened it and found that this was given to us to step up our dedication and also motivate us. It had a book which gave us details of the prizes we would get if we were to be the lucky ones. We would get:

1. A Lifetime supply of water.
2. Good jobs for all the winners. And lucky one would get the prestigious position of the Minister of the Palace.
3. A beautiful, big mansion.
4. Hundred thousand levens (one leven is fifty dollars).
5. One cute Lowchen puppy with a big dog house for it to live in, along with a five-year food supply for the dog.
6. Three vouchers of one thousand each of the best brands of clothes, accessories, sports, etc.

I never, in my wildest dreams, imagined I could get this luck. But in a moment of reflex, I got jittery about the whole process. The prizes then didn't seem important! I closed the bag and opened the small zip. In that, I found a packet of tablets. I had heard about them but had never consumed one. It is a tablet which you have to just put at the tip of your tongue, and it starts melting with the saliva of the mouth. As it melts, it turns into the flavor you desire. One is sufficient to fill you up and to even relieve your thirst. This was provided as a supplement to food and water, keeping the scarcity of water in mind.

Mamothimo started shouting, 'Only ten minutes left for our plane to leave, so pack your bags as soon as possible, and we shall leave to be in time for the aircraft.'

I packed my bag and hung it on my back. We all lined up behind Mamothimo with our hearts in our mouth and left for our plane with our passports in our hands. We boarded the craft, and an announcement said, 'The flight is a three-hour journey, and in an hour, we shall provide you with our special in-flight dinner—planned and cooked specially for you all as a Royal Feast by the world's finest chefs. You can watch television, but before that, be sure to tighten you seat belts.' The voice of the announcer sounded soft and calm, but at the same time, it was dominating and bossy. Nothing could calm our nerves as the upcoming uncertainty was gnawing our interiors. I did not want to think of anything at that moment and just wanted to feel secure, ready, and set for my upcoming task. Deep down, I knew that I had to emerge as a winner, for I could not let my parents down—not for being unable to give them lifetime supply of water but because time and again, I had been imagining their face on hearing about the news of me not having survived. That thought, the imaginary expression of their faces, the anxiety they would face, and the helplessness that they would feel, all these things combined did not wear me down but gave me the courage and strength to face all the challenges that this 'one of a kind' dare had in store for me. And the silver lining was 'water', especially for my dearest family. That motivation was very strong.

CHAPTER 5

I followed the announcer's directions, for it was all for our good and safety. I realized that it was a chartered flight for only us. But shortly, I figured it was a private aircraft. The feeling of great pride and superiority crept inside me because for a lower-middle-class person like me, it was a lifetime opportunity, or maybe a dream I can call it, which would never get fulfilled! And being there on that private jet elated my satiation for a while. But the jitters of what would happen in the next few days and the very thought of why and how I was in this private jet diluted away all the pride!

The TV was the world's first curved TV. It was awesome and huge. Again, the feeling of 'importance' swept in. I immediately switched it on. In the Northern part of Africa, the series 'Seven's Got Six' is aired daily, and I was used to watching it every day. In that serial, there is a girl named Seven, who has six brothers, and, thus, she would always feel like the odd one out. Unluckily, she was the eldest and had the responsibility of her ferocious brothers after their parents had separated. I really like the way they have elaborated on the girl's emotions and the way she looks after them. I thought I had missed it, but luckily, I could see it on the flight as well. I felt euphoric for not having missed it, as though I had reached home safe after all the days in the palace, back to my family, back in my mum's arms. I watched the serial for almost an hour before I could realize that it was already dinner time, wherein we were served rice and Thai curry. Apart from that, we had an option between Chinese and Italian cuisines, with the rice and Thai curry being mandatory. For drinks, water was compulsory, and there was a pick between Coke, Sprite, Fanta, and Caprioska. For desserts, cake was obligatory and choices between ice-cream and jelly. The ice-cream counter had all kinds of scrumptious flavours and delicacies. For main course, as an option between Chinese and Italian, I picked Chinese since I have an intense fondness for Chinese Hakka Noodles and other savouries made out of A-Ji-No-Moto, their main ingredient, maybe because it sends a nerve satisfying message to the brain, giving a sense of fulfillment. For the drinks, among Coke, Fanta, and Sprite, again I opted for the most brain-enticing one due to its high caffeine content—Coke. As an option between ice-cream and jelly, I ate ice-cream since there were many delicious and mouth-watering flavours, and also that it had an unlimited serving. So many enticing things in my platter were indeed a luxury for me, and at that moment, I couldn't have asked for more because many days after landing, we would be on a tablet diet. Shortly though, an announcement was heard again, 'We shall reach in one and a half hour. Therefore, please hurry up with your food. And if you wish, you can even take a nap, as sleep will evade you in INSTATUSQUO.' I gobbled up all the yummy things in my plate and snoozed off.

This was just an interesting beginning to woo us into a zone of hopelessness and uncertainty. We were given a feeling of temporary elation as nobody knew what was next.

CHAPTER 6

Fifteen minutes later, I was up! I witnessed a terrible dream on the flight, or I must say almost a nightmare. I was dead in the palace. The scary and shuddery dream shook me from within, and I shouted on the top of my voice and yelled my lungs out. Sminka Flear, who was beside me, woke up and stood over her seat. She looked like a white scary ghost to me after that shivery dream. She shrieked, 'Is there any bug under me?' She looked anxious, but still, I felt like replying to her, 'Bug? Under you? There's no bug under you. You are bugging me!" Mamothimo came running towards us and asked, 'Child, do you want some water?' My restlessness kind of faded, listening to his consoling voice, and I replied, 'No, I feel better now.' He seemed to be kind and reflected my actions.

We packed our bags and reached in about five minutes from then. After landing and picking our bags, we checked out and departed from the airport. There were five cars, which had come to pick us up. I was in total awe of the convoy of luxury cars that were lined up there right in front of us. Suddenly, a dog came and stood beside me. For as inquisitive as I am for every little thing, I enquired about its whereabouts. Mamothimo told me that he was one of us, a part of the team. Hearing that made me feel nice in a way, but then the thought flooded up—'One of us? Is he also going to perish like most of us?' Soon, I got distracted again as the cars pulled up, and we started loading our luggage in them and getting in to move on.

The first car was a Black BMW-X5, an eight-seater SUV, stylish, and humongous, which took Sminka, Midget, Fosenca, Demoler, Heath, Fleenker, and Flinco. The second car was a black Audi- Q7, again an eight-seater passenger vehicle, spacious, colossal, and swanky. It accommodated Kensia, Lonta, Lomus, Lenrica, Tencia, Himlona, and Shaskes. The third car, was a real beauty and larger than life, Monroe Limo, a grand Limousine. Looking at it, I silently wished I could grab a place in it, which luckily I did, so the limousine threw its doors open for Trithpil, Tonthany, Waliom, Mamothimo,

Facancia, Sester, and me. Another exhilarating experience, one more emotion of being fortunate, gave the edge of being a winner and posing in that majestic vehicle, all my fears swept away.

I don't know about the other two cars since I left before others could sit—left and lost in my fascinating beauty world. We swished and swashed and enjoyed in the car. It took us almost an hour to reach our destination because it was far, but the journey was pleasant, nice, and opulent.

Again, a thought flashed. 'These were our last happy moments, but I wanted to make the best out of even those ten to fifteen minutes I had probably for life to end.' My positivity always gave me a good feel, and circumstances seemed fruitful, but my negativity gave me less hope for survival. We reached and were told to hop out of our cars and to stand in a row facing the Palace of Statements, probably an end to our lives or maybe a new beginning . . .

CHAPTER 7

The Palace of Statements, with its empowering façade, was so close yet seemed so far. Close, physically, but far because of our fears.

It seemed that the palace was designed in a way that half of it had daylight and the other half was entrenched in darkness. It also looked very technologically innovative.

Though intriguing, it also wore a horrifying look. One of the drivers said, 'In five minutes, you will enter the majestic palace.' This is the moment. The moment we all are here for. And after which, nobody knew of how many more moments each would have. Suddenly, everyone around seemed to be like family to me, each and every person a part of it. On their faces, I could read that though they were looking forward to enter that palace, the fear of not being able to come out of it was also prevailing. I had a strong feeling that somebody, one of us, would surrender and shout, 'No, I cannot do it.' But to my great astonishment, nobody did. We all stood there straight, bold, daring, valiant, and gritty. The optimism showed in every single person's body language. Each one present there thought that he or she would be the one coming out of the palace as a winner. I think this positive approach allowed everybody to have the fortitude to face the challenge. Everybody had a reason to come out of it. Being with my parents and making them proud was mine.

Mamothimo gave everyone a watch. He had made sure that all the watches he was distributing showed exactly the same time. We all wore it and proceeded to meet each other. I walked towards Tonthany Brusoe, he was a chariot rider's son, but he was the most pro-active. He was very brave too. He asked me, 'Are you prepared?' I told him, 'Yes, of course', and we both started laughing at our manner of communication. As I moved around, a small girl named Lonta started following me. She was very cute and seemed to be about three years old. Her hair was dark brown, French braided into two, which highlighted her face, and her black expressive eyes spoke volumes. She wore a beautiful blue dress and was so adorable that I couldn't help myself from lifting her in my arms. She pointed towards Facancia, so I moved in that direction. Facancia had another cute girl in her hands who looked exactly like Lonta. It took me time to realize that they were twins. Facancia was Sminka's twin. We all, in the town, knew their story. They seem to be great sisters. Facancia looked courageous and seemed to be studious and scholarly, for she was wearing black rimmed spectacles. She had blue eyes and red hair. She was boney, and her hair was neatly plaited in a Dutch braid. Her fair skin looked splendid. Midget Kill, a young adult, also a contestant, who was nice and kind to people, walked towards Facancia and handed her a rose. She was full of wrath and smacked the rose on his face. He presented it to me. I didn't like it either, but I didn't want to be impolite to him, so I accepted it. The drivers told us, 'Get ready. And at the start of each hour, death will summon one person. So as you'll enter, the fatal clock strikes. Don't be scared. Be brave. Best of luck to all of you. Don't lose your fate. Power and courage can make you a winner. Be mettlesome and start off with one good reason to be back.'

CHAPTER 8

We entered very cautiously. Mamothimo went in prototypically first, and Heath was the last one to walk in—for what reason, none of us figured. As she perforated in, a cutter went through her entire body from the side panels of the palace entrance, exactly like how sugarcane goes through the juice extractor. She took less than a second to be stone dead, giving her no time to even utter a shrill cry. Her blood was all over Fleenker who walked right ahead of her. Drenched in blood all over, she looked like a dead person herself. It took us awhile to actually relate and understand what exactly had transpired. Fleenker was speechless. Plainly, her body felt benumbed, not only due to the blood all over her but also because she could very well comprehend that she got saved by a matter of a few seconds. The importance of an 'iota of luck' seeped into her. She felt a sense of relief as well as trauma. Every cell squirmed after this experience.

Lonta started wailing. I was afraid too, but looking at Lonta and Fonsenca, I must say that we all had to pull ourselves together. Being such a small, merely out-of-the-womb child, who must've probably left her parents to be on her own for the very first time, it was the biggest and most daring thing for any of us to imagine. I could not understand how this child must have left her house for this. Maybe she was too small to even know the atrocities she was going to face, but her parents? How could they have dared to let go of their little angel like that!

Seeing Lonta and Fonsenca and imagining all that, we knew that we had to help rather than being hopeless ourselves. We went ahead abandoning Heath's body behind. We kept walking hither thither for ten minutes but couldn't find anything. Then a voice came from the background, 'I'm the villain here. I can kill anyone at free will, but every hour, I'll make your mission tough. If you wish to save yourself, you need to find the clues laid out throughout the palace. These clues can be in the form of words, things—anything. I'm not saying more than this because you have to work for it yourself, so get going people and expect no mercy. This is the mission where your spontaneity decides if you can progress ahead.'

Ghost?! With eyes wide open in astonishment, we looked at each other because this wasn't what any of us was expecting. We had not in our wildest thoughts expected that there would be a ghost in the palace who would be our guiding, killing, and saving role model!

Every word spoken by the so-called ghost was ringing in my ears as though somebody had just killed me right there and then was pretending to help me get alive again.

Everybody was panic stricken and unable to move. We knew we had to move and start searching for the clues, but somehow, our brains were too exhausted to get our limbs moving. At that moment, Fleenker shouted, 'Clues', and soon, we got back to our cognizance and realized that we didn't have much time since the ghost had used the word 'clues'—thanks to Fleenker for that. We realized we had to start working immediately. We started searching here and there but couldn't find a thing. I took a quick glimpse at my wrist watch. The time was 6.30 a.m. I screamed, 'Only half an hour is left for the second death!'

Mamothimo took charge again and said, 'We have to split into groups. Otherwise, we won't be able to find a single clue.' We all agreed to this suggestion and divided ourselves in five groups consisting of six members each. I was in group number two with Facancia, Lonta, Fonsenca Sminka, and Fleenker. Mamothimo suggested that the leader should hold the communicating device. I was my group's leader, so I held it. All this took up fifteen minutes, and now, the time was 6.45 a.m. All the groups started walking in different directions to search for the clues. Our group found one clue, but before we realized it's a clue, it was already 7.00 a.m.

The clue we found was lying on a small table, in a transparent box. It wouldn't just give way when we realized it needed a password to open the box, and when someone said the word 'statement', It just popped open. I was sure it was the word 'statement' because our entire mission and deal was based on that. I happened to look up at the roof and saw a huge, heavy log falling down from the roof, right towards Fleenker. I shouted at the top of my voice, 'Fleenker, move!'

CHAPTER 9

She didn't move! She had less than a fraction of a second to do that, so how could she?! But I wished she had. The log came down like a ton of bricks over her, crushing her body, splashing blood all over, and she lay there lifeless. Gory sight! We wondered who was responsible for these acts. Who was timing all this? Who was the architect?

I called Mamothimo on the communicating device and told him about the loss of Fleenker. He said, 'It's OK. Anyway, I found a clue.' 'So did I', I told him. 'Let's meet at the same place from where we scattered', said he. It was 7.15 a.m. We reached the meeting point simultaneously, with our groups. I went up to Mamothimo, hugged him, and told him, 'I don't want any more people dying because of our stupidity of not being able to work on time. We can't do this in this manner. We have to work together to be able to save our fellow mates or maybe to save ourselves.'Mamothimo was moved. He replied, 'Fine, for you we shall call all the groups again and become one big gang. I agree we need to be together to solve the clues.' He called all the groups back there through the communicating device, and by the time we reunited, it was 7.30 a.m. We wasted quite some time in the first two hours!

Only two clues were found, one by Mamothimo and the other by my group! Both were in the form of chits. I opened my chit and read it out aloud, 'The meet of the world is one more death.' Nobody understood what that meant. We looked at Mamothimo to read out his clue, which he did. It said, 'The death is the WIN.' None of us understood what the other one meant too, except for Mamothimo. That's what he said, 'I understand this clue very well. Once Hanah dies, we will win, and it's final.' Hanah screamed, feeling nervous and scared. 'Why only me?' Mamothimo explained, 'Hanah in Trithon, the language of the ghosts means death. So Hanah's death is the win for us, which exactly means that when you die Hanah, we will win.'

Hanah showed a lot of courage. She replied, 'I'll give my life to make you all win. I'll die, and I shall feel proud to do that.' Hesitatingly, I said, 'But the villain might have a plan to save you, or maybe Mamothimo has encrypted the clue wrongly. Let's not start judging.'

'Let's just work before another death occurs', said Tonthany. I exclaimed, 'After the first two deaths and after encrypting the chit as Mamothimo did, isn't it clear that everything is pre-decided? I mean, it seems as though the rascal has already decided who will die and how!'

Everybody listened to my point silently and nodded their heads in affirmation. Mamothimo then replied, 'Yes, child, up until now, it does seem like that, maybe because we haven't been able to crack any clue yet. Once we move the right way and know exactly what to do, we might be able to save lives.' We nodded our heads in agreement. But Lomus spoke up and said, 'Everything is pre-decided, so how do we even save lives and rescue our fellow team mates?' Then I said, 'Lomus, there is only one way we can save everyone, and that is by working fast. Then why not? Now stop getting confused, and let's start working on the task we are assigned.'

I looked at my watch again. It was 8 a.m. Immediately, before I could utter a word about the time, a crack of a head was heard! We all looked around aghast because everyone was expecting the unexpected . . .

CHAPTER 10

Demoler had fallen and hurt himself severely. His head had cracked open. How? None of us knew. It was bleeding all over, and we could literally see the brain in its skeletal form. It was a disgusting and a petrifying sight. Mamothimo quickly opened his first-aid kit. He removed his stethoscope and bent down with his ear on Demoler's chest. He didn't hear a single heartbeat. There was stoic silence. With a heavy heart, he announced, 'He's dead.'Demoler's wife, Sester, came running towards him, crying, and sobbing inconsolably. She started talking to her husband's dead body. 'What's the point of me living without you. I loved you even more than myself.' She sniveled even louder. 'You were going to be a father! Yes, that's true. I'm pregnant, but now it's futile. I want to exit from this planet. I can't think of life without you. I accept death, and that's all I want now.'

Taking her emotions in control, she looked at Hanah and said vehemently, 'You were supposed to die right? Then why did my husband die?' Hanah had no words.

We all felt sorry for Sester, not only because her loss was too big for her to accept but also because she was carrying. A pregnant woman, having so much courage to participate in a challenge and see such horrid deaths was not at all easy because of the hormonal changes a woman's body goes through during such a period. She had been really brave, and I could understand her grief of not wanting to live anymore. Mamothimo was trying to pacify her, but she was totally inconsolable.

My thoughts had started wandering again, thinking repeatedly of the ruthless death of Demoler, about how everything was pre-planned, and that how we were too helpless to do anything. I shouted in anger, 'This is not a competition. Everything here is planned, and we are all victims of this illusionary "Game of Chance" because there's no chance here. There's only death—planned and crafted for each one of us and, that too, in the most horrific ways.'

Everybody looked at me while I spoke, and I could read it in their eyes that they agreed with me. But nobody had any words to utter. I felt as though I spoke ineffectually. The only thing I achieved after the huge outcry was that Sester had stopped crying and was now somewhat under control. That in itself was a bit of an achievement as we could now proceed ahead to get working. She was so frightened at the thought of dying that she said, 'Now, no more. I want to leave this fatal palace where my husband was tortured to death.' But Mamothimo said, 'You just can't be selfish. You are also a tiny hope for the entire team even though you have wasted an entire hour. If you leave all of us and go, it means not even one of us would get what we have come here for. Think of the three disastrous deaths. Those people who were courageous enough to die for others, for the town, died for no sense? For nothing? If not Heath and Fleenker, at least care for your husband, Demoler, who has just wished for you to survive.'

Tonthany came up to me and held my hand. He said, 'Don't worry. We still have to work here. This is just one side of the palace wherein it's dark and ugly. Maybe the other side is better because its day there, so maybe the experiences there will be brighter. Let's hope for the best. Keep yourself calm or we can achieve nothing.' He was kind and courageous. His soothing words felt like a blessing at that moment. I nodded. He smiled. We shook hands and became partners in business.

It was 8.45 a.m. already—just fifteen minutes away from another death. The only person we could blame for being unable to work on another clue was Sester, but we could understand her plea and didn't want her to die as she was bringing a child to this world. I didn't know whether I wanted to be there for Sester, consoling and pacifying her or to get working on another clue to save one life. Just at that time, Tonthany said to me, 'If the others can't come, at least we could go and search for clues before another death occurs.' I agreed with him, and we both set off to look for some hint. In our heads, we were thanking God that at least we had ten minutes to look for a clue. But every minute seemed to pass away like a second. We knew we had very little time, but even more than that, time was flying like a bird that flies when its children are starving for food, and it is desperately searching for nourishment to take to the nest. I understood the importance of every single second at that time because I knew we could not lose out on a single one. Helpless and clueless as we were, not knowing where to head and what to look for, we were prancing here and there, all around, to find something at least, which could lead us to something big. Soon, as they say, 'Determination leads to success', I found myself standing in front of Toader Course. Toader Course is a famous painting. We found a clue right there. I looked at the time. It was 9.00 a.m. already!

CHAPTER 11

Since Tonthany and I were alive, we understood that somebody else from the group had passed away. I quickly grabbed the clue from the Toader Course, and we both rushed towards the place where our fellow colleagues were waiting. I was sure that a death had definitely occurred since we were past that stipulated time, but I didn't expect it to be that dreadful. An axe came flying from nowhere and hit Tases on his stomach. The hit was so powerful that his vital organs had popped out of the body. There was no chance of survival, and this 'scum of the earth' made sure that each time the target hits the bull's eye. By now, we should have been used to seeing dead bodies and blood scattered around everywhere and people sobbing hopelessly, but we also had a heart, which could not bear the ruthless thought of someone of our group, who we know so well or looked up to dies in just a very dark hour of life. Each time, the dead body was worse than the previous time. Though I could understand Sester's emotions and position at that time, I also felt terrible for Tases and emphasized his presence in my head. The chit we found proved us as a dedicated member of the group. I handed over the chit to Mamothimo, indicating that Tonthany and I had found a clue while Sester was wailing at the loss of her husband, and everyone else in group was trying to console her. Sester understood her mistake and stopped crying and said, 'Let's check that clue without wasting another second', but she didn't realize that she had wasted an entire hour. Mamothimo opened it. It had a sign pointing left ward.

All of us started to proceed in the direction of the arrow and kept following it. Lonta and ten others were behind me. They saw a clue right behind me. It was sparkling in the light. Lonta yelled, 'A clue!' We all turned towards her as she stood there holding it. She was enthusiastic about opening it, so we gave her the honors. She opened it and gave it to me as she was too young to fathom reading it out. I grasped it and read it out aloud, 'North, East, South, West—Flinco is the next person to be dead.'

Everybody looked at Flinco with sympathetic eyes. Her face had turned unimaginably small, and the fright of death made her entire body tremble and shiver, leaving her unable to utter a single word. The look on her newly turned puny face and blank look in her eyes were enough to analyze her state of mind. She looked up at the roof and then at all the sides to see what weapon was coming from which side to kill her. She kind of accepted the imaginary weapon and knelt down on her knees, saying her last prayers with hands joined together.

I quickly looked at my watch, which showed 9.45 a.m. I said in a rush, 'Hurry! We need to save Flinco. Do something!' Mamothimo said, 'Guard! Let's guard her and protect her from all sides, even from top.' We all agreed. Tonthany continued, 'Not a single space should be left open for anything to go through, no arrow, no axe—nothing that can kill should be able to pass through.' Quickly, we all got into action. Tencia and Sester surrounded her from the sides. I pulled up in front of her, and Tonthany hurried behind her and so on. We made a human pyramid with extra safety all around and over Flinco, leaving no chance for the wrongdoer to kill her.

I thought to myself *Thus we could prove her destiny wrong, but Flinco will definitely die, as the rogue has said that!* And my sixth sense could also perceive Flinco's death!

As we rallied around Flinco, she was muttering under her breath, 'I know I am going to die as the bad man said so. But even if I die, I want to live in your hearts. I want you'll to win. Our mission should succeed, and we all should achieve it, even if many of us perish. We are a team, and we must prove it. My last wish is that you'll just tell my parents that I only died for them and have also lived these twenty years of my life only for them and not for anyone else.' We were so stressed about her protection that half of us didn't register what she said.

CHAPTER 12

I twisted my wrist a bit to look at the time, making sure to keep the balance of the pyramid intact. To my utmost shock, the time was 10.01 a.m. I shrieked, 'It's one past ten, and Flinco isn't dead. Yes, we have done it.' Mamothimo said, 'Let's descend then and celebrate.' We all got down very carefully feeling victorious that we were able to save Flinco and that we had outlived the rogue's words as none of us had died at this hour. But this happiness of victory was short-lived. As we all descended and made way, we saw that Flinco was dead due to exhaustion. We had packed her up way too well, and, thus, there was no space for even air to get in. With lack of oxygen and having only exhaled carbon dioxide in the atmosphere around her, she collapsed and died due to claustrophobia. Something we didn't expect!

We felt extremely melancholic and also angry at our own doing. How could we not be aware of our own actions? Our conscience was humiliated by our own identities, and now we were in no position to react to Flinco's death. Mamothimo once again took control over the moment and said, 'It was no use queuing up. It's vividly clear now that we cannot save any lives here. Rather we should focus on finding "The Statement" for which we all are here, risking our lives. The wrongdoer is trying to distract us from our mission by dropping clues on the next fatality. We can in no way change that, so let's work on finding "The Statement".'

Sester started yelling and crying. 'I don't want to find anything. I just want my husband back. If not, I want to die myself. How can he die leaving me alone?'

Mamothimo got really angry this time and said, 'Poor thing Tases died because of you, you mad girl. And look at you! You are still crying for your husband?! Everyone loses someone out here. Even I have come to lose something very precious to me—'He became quiet rather quickly before completing the sentence as though he was hiding something important. But at that moment, nobody cared to question him about his incomplete sentence.

He then said, 'I am going in search of "The Statement", and I hope that everybody here has understood that that's what is expected out of us. Whoever agrees with me, please follow, and the ones who wish to wail over the dead may stay here and do so.'

All of us, including Sester, followed Mamothimo's decision and flung our steps towards his.

Not too far away, we saw Carper's painting hung on the wall. The only thing different about it was that it was labeled. A Carper's painting labeled? I immediately could understand that there was something in that, but I couldn't fathom what that was. A quick look at my watch, and it was 10.35 a.m.

I wasn't happy at all. My nerves tightened, and my muscles felt sore, just as much was needed to make me feel that this is the end of my life. Everything seemed like the end of the world to me, and I started feeling quite pessimistic, unlike how I was feeling while entering the palace. My parents' faces flashed in front of my eyes, and I couldn't show them my face. They were smiling, I smiled back, and their faces disappeared. That was enough to bring me back to the moment and to do what was important then.

The label was in fact a clue but was jumbled up. It took us a few minutes to put the words in place, and the only sensible sentence that came out of it was, 'How could someone be as dumb as Trinka? She should be erased from the face of this earth.' We were not sure that we had made the correct sentence out of the jumbled letters, but putting them together with the given pointers, this was all we got out of it. So it was quite clear that Trinka was the next one to die. We looked at her. She stood calm and peaceful. We began hurrying up to do something to save her, but she immediately stepped back and said, 'It's really no use at all. I shall die anyway if the ghost has decided to do so, just as Flinco did. And it's really fine with me.'

What she said did make sense, and frankly, there was actually no way in which we could help her. We stayed there quiet. She asked us to carry on and not to waste time finding 'The Statement'. But none of us had the heart to leave her there to die all alone. We had indeed evolved; despite seeing so many deaths, we were still human, and our emotions had not died.

Trinka, a young soul with a beautiful heart, wanted to die herself and didn't want us saving her, for she was concerned about the welfare of the team. She told us to move on because we wouldn't want to see her dead body. But none of us had the heart to do so. She was a motivation to all as she taught us an important life lesson. We thought of everyone who had died, and when we opened our eyes, we all sat there in a circle, holding each other's hands and praying.

A twist of the wrist to check the time and it was 11.00 a.m.

CHAPTER 13

I dared to take a glimpse around. 'Trinka is dead.' I gulped my breath and was petrified this time. The target was her beautiful blue eyes. With sharp spikes in her eyes, her body lay there lifeless. I was wondering why she didn't even shriek or shout when the horrendous spikes got into her eyes. For that matter, as I sat there relating to the deaths, I evaluated that all the people who had succumbed fatally at the palace didn't react verbally. Their bodies were found mutilated, killed in the most ruthless way ever, but still none of them had wailed even a bit!

As everybody was already prepared for Trinka's death, they all started proceeding, and I followed suit. We all walked right behind Mamothimo, and I'm sure each one of us was wondering who the next target would be.

The palace was the darkest place I had ever seen. The only hope I had was my torch. If that stopped working, then we would feel trapped. It was pitch dark. Nothing in front of us was visible. The walls were covered with famous paintings. As we walked through, we could imagine how affluent the owner was to be able to afford such expensive paintings like Monalisa replica and paintings made by Picasso and Van Gogh. We were lucky to be able to see such fabulous pieces of art. The floor was soft at some places and super hard at some. It was dented, and anything on it seemed like some expensive alloy of brass or gold. Less than forty steps away, Himlona found our next clue laid on the ground. It was a chit again. She read out the contents, 'French'. Nobody understood what the clue really meant or what it was trying to point out to. We spent a few minutes working on that clue, trying to analyse its meaning in the situation. But we couldn't place it anywhere in the current scenario, so we decided to move on for something more.

Time was passing by! Every second seemed heavy, indicating the hour ending soon and facing another teammate's death. The anxiety and uneasiness could be gaited in every person's body—the way we walked, spoke, looked around, even breathed, everything.

I was counting each minute precisely, just to calculate how much more time we had. Now it was 11.50 a.m. just as Sminka found an envelope lying protectively on a wooden table, well lit for visibility. It sure was a clue. She picked it up, opened the envelope, and removed the letter out of it which read, 'Leader, leader, be my killer?!'

Before we could understand or even talk about the letter, I noticed a sudden change in Mamothimo. Others were preoccupied discussing about the clue and its indication, but I quietly gestured to them to stay quiet and look at Mamothimo. His body had stiffened, his eyes had turned red, his eyebrows scrunched together as if he was concentrating, and his limbs seemed fixed to the ground as though immovable. It was clear that Mamothimo had been hypnotized. But by whom? There was nobody around who would do it because the hypnotizer had to look into the victim's eyes in order to hypnotize him. It was either the 'malified architect' who could do it, or then maybe he was hypnotized automatically. In a sluggish voice, he yelled, 'I'm your killer, daughter, son. Ha ha ha! I'm her killer! I'm her killer! I'm her killer! I'm going to kill you all. You all will be dead because I want to kill.'

Everybody around was perturbed looking at Mamothimo. They started fighting and arguing about how Mamothimo could want to kill his own teammates, and how he can think of killing when they were all suffering. People started panicking and were really scared of Mamothimo. The very fact that he was not moving a single limb or any other body part and not behaving mad made it obvious that he was not his usual self. I pointed that out to the others, with Tonthany's help, and only then did they calm down a bit. They finally, after a lot of effort, understood that something was wrong with Mamothimo. But what he would do in that state? None of us could judge!

I was in deep thought, a bit scared that Mamothimo, our leader, under hypnotic influence, might take one of his teammates life or might kill everybody. More than that, I was also worried that Mamothimo might never be fine again ever!

Mamothimo was out of his senses. We all could feel it, especially when he approached me. I was panic-stricken that it is me who is going to die at 12.00 noon.

That only created fear in my mind, and all I could think was, 'Why only me?' This was just my fear which stopped me from reacting. Facancia was my savior, and bravely, she called out, 'Come kill me, not her.' He said in an absolutely diffident voice, 'No, she is the best in the team, and, thus, she is the only one who deserves death.' Trientika, one of the bravest of the team, pushed me away, and then Mamothimo held her neck in order to kill her, and that saved me.

CHAPTER 14

With fear in my heart and hope in my mind, I looked around to check whether Trientika was dead. Fear that Mamothimo has killed her and hope that he was all right because at such a crucial time, I could not afford to lose him. In utter agnosticism, I witnessed that Mamothimo had ripped off Trientika's throat, the same hands that were going to kill me! After the action, he stood there simply straight, without any agony, fear, or even disgust at himself. Trientika lay dead on the floor. She saved my life, and I was extremely sad at her demise, as though someone like my long lost sister had died. It was a horrible sight. Everybody stared at her and at Mamothimo, feeling appalled at the entire scenario.

It was clear that Mamothimo was the executioner at this moment, but it was not him. He was doing it under the control of outside force; thus, he was innocent. The immediate need of the moment was to get Mamothimo back to his original self before he could cause any more harm. 'Let's do something to get him back,' said Tonthany. Everybody agreed and tried to do different things to Mamothimo like screeching at him, shaking him up, even hitting him hard, but Mamothimo was still in the same form, escalating the fear and hopelessness in us.

Mamothimo had fainted. He was unconscious after killing one sweet girl who saved my life. People like Midget and Sester said, 'If he doesn't get up in ten minutes, we will leave him and go to find the statement. I felt like strangling Sester, but I controlled my emotions. She was the reason for Tases's death and also for the delay of an hour, and now for a person who was so gentle and nice, barring a very good leader, how could she even think of ignoring his predicament? More than the scoundrel, I felt she was the villain of my story. I said, 'People say if you make an unconscious person smell a shoe, he or she gets up instantly. That is not possible in our case, but if we have something stinky, maybe we can—'Midget interrupted and said, 'No, Riya, we can't because there is no such thing.' He was right, but he didn't even want to try! After two hopeless minutes passed, Mamothimo asked, 'Why are we waiting? What just happened? I am blank about everything.' We were delighted that our leader was back and normal. I wanted to give it back to Sester and tell her that she was wrong, but we had no time to waste on her. With a heavy heart, we told Mamothimo about what had happened. He didn't know a thing about how Trientika had died, and when he got to know that he was responsible for her death, he was aghast. Shameful and sorry as he was, he dropped down on the floor and said, 'I was here, as your leader, to help you all and guide you all. Not to do this! I can never forgive myself for this, and all I deserve for this ghastly act is death.' I immediately interrupted, 'Whatever has happened was not your fault. You did it under hypnotic influence, and, thus, you cannot be blamed for it. You were just a weapon used by the perpetrator, not the murderer yourself.' Mamothimo got up and gave me a hug followed by a kiss on the forehead and said, 'Child, I wish I hadn't been the weapon.' Before he could say anything, I again interrupted, 'Let's get moving without wasting any more time. None of us are upset with you. In fact, we are glad that our leader is back with us.' And we walked ahead.

As we moved on, I couldn't help myself from thinking about the wrongdoer and then suddenly reminisced stories about such characters that I had read and heard as a child.

The story behind entering the palace was:

One day, a huge chariot arrived at Incognito. It had a bright red curtain made up of rich velvet and seemed like behind it there were loads of presents. I didn't know why and what it was for, and the inquisitiveness in me led me to the roads of spying. Me and my friend Lien, who is like a sister to me, set off on our journey to find out more. Lien had three elder brothers and one younger sister. They were quite nice, except her eldest brother who was really arrogant and bossy. Lien and I studied in the same class, and we were best friends since kindergarten and, thus, very close. Our 'what I want to be when I grow up' was always 'explorers' and 'spies', and that's how we gelled so well. That's why we practiced spying when we found something fishy. So that day, we knew that we needed to follow that chariot. Behind the bushes, we walked so that people didn't realize that we were actually spying on the mystery chariot. Once they stopped near the entrance of the Royal Palace, we walked behind them with nimble feet. They entered the palace. We entered in there too, from the back door, which we had discovered a few months ago. They were sitting on the dining table. Food of all different cuisines was laid on the marbled table. The emperor or king of some other kingdom seemed to be the one our king was speaking to. The other emperor presented the royal gifts and started speaking, 'I have not come here to have lunch with you. I have come here to challenge you.' Our king listened plainly. He continued, 'I have heard that the abundance of water has hit this town badly, and people here are in dire need of it. So much that they are willing to do anything for it!' Our king said, 'What do you mean? Are you trying to imply that I am not a good king?' The emperor responded, 'No! I have no such intention, but I do understand that it is tough to provide water to everybody due to its scarcity, and unfortunately, it is a necessity! I am the king of Instatusquo, and I have come here to challenge you and your kingdom. It is a tough challenge and a bit complicated but not impossible. In my kingdom, there is a palace called the 'Palace of Statements'. Its interior and exterior is designed in such a way that half of it portrays the sunlight that creates the beautiful daytime, and the other half depicts the night, which people fear of. My challenge to you is to send thirty-one people to this palace. Each hour, one person dies, and all they have to do is find a statement—a statement which can save lives.' The King of Incognito hesitated and asked, 'What will we get?' You will get my kingdom, Instatusquo, and a thousand Levens. All the contenders would get a lifetime supply of water, and the ones who survived and succeeded would get water and a few more things everyone wishes for but doesn't get easily. And if these people are unable to bring the statement, you will have to give me your kingdom and a thousand Levens. It is a fair deal.' Our King got scared and vulnerable and so were we, but next what happened was unimaginable for us. Our king saw two eyes staring at him. These were my eyes. He cried out loudly. 'Come out, you spies!' We both, Lien and I, walked up in front of him with shivering bodies and confused minds. He asked, 'You two have entered in here without any permission which is next to impossible as per me. Details of that I shall take from you soon. For now, did you two dare to hear the entire conversation?' We replied hesitatingly, 'Yes.' Now, if we make this deal, one of these two daring girls have to step in death's doors as a punishment', said he. I responded immediately, 'Please send me to the Palace of Statements as my family requires water. Please, sir, please do not send my soulmate, Lien, for she is suffering from blood cancer, and her treatment is in progress.' The king accepted the offer from the King of Instatusquo, only by looking at the sparkle in my eyes, which exuded confidence, and he was sure that I would come out of this victorious! Lien was upset as she couldn't afford losing her best friend. I promised her that I would succeed, which seemed difficult only to her then. But now I too am scared that I probably won't!

'There's no other clue to be seen anywhere', said an exhausted voice. It was Lomus Freelter. Abruptly, I heard a sound from the south, and immediately, I figured that the clue has just been hidden by the villain or rather by Mr Lonedon Englond. I shouted, 'The owner, the clue, everything is there—behind. We need to go back towards it. I'm sure there's something laid, which we have overlooked. Or probably that chap has purposely put it after we crossed the place. He wants us to turn back. He's the ghost, the owner of this palace. Let's quickly go towards it.'

It was indeed too late. Just one minute was left for the next kill. I saw it and shouted out as loud as I could. 'Sester', but it was no use!

CHAPTER 15

In the spur of the moment, Sester was dead. I saw her die. The hands came to her throat and strangled her to death in less than two seconds. These 'hands' were anonymous, belonging to whom that nobody knew. They just sprung out in the air, came up to her, and killed her! The sight was scary, and I was literally trembling. Everytime after a fatal occurrence, I imagined myself in the situation and wondered what lay in store for me, and it traumatized me, but this lifeless body of Sester further aggravated my psyche.

Sester was a trouble maker, kind of a killer herself. She was giving us too much grief in there. Thus, we were not too sad about her death despite her being pregnant.

Catching hold of my strength, with a deep breath, I continued walking in that palace, trying to forget about those murderous 'hands', trying to look out for another clue, and hoping to get it soon. Time was passing too fast, and still each second felt like an hour. Every single moment in that palace was getting more and more laborious, and I was desperately desiring a quick end, or at least a 'pause'. 'End' in the form of end of the challenge or even 'end' in the form of end of myself. Yes, by now, I was too fatigued—mentally, physically, and emotionally that I wished for any kind of 'end' soon.

A boon at that very moment, Trithphill said in a vehement outcry, 'That's a clue. That board. Look there.' Pointing at a black-coloured board, she continued, 'Go towards the north—that's what it says.'

We all looked at it and restlessly walked towards the direction of the board and proceeded northward. *Hopefully we will find something in time,* I thought. As we went a few steps northward, maybe around thirty steps or so, we reached a place having a totally different atmosphere. It was a semi arid region of the palace. Mamothimo exclaimed, 'We have entered the day side of the palace.'

'This is much better,' mumbled Fonsenca. 'Look, we can't go backwards. We actually can't go to the night side again! This is like a trap. It's a maze', said Tonthany. I shrieked. 'That means that nobody will be able to reach back to Sester's body.' Nobody cared. They all were too curious to look around and understand the new place to know what it had in store for everyone.

The day side seemed much better than the night, as it infused positive energy into us and made us feel much better though we knew that half the mission is over, meaning only half the deaths! And we would have to see many more! But at the same time, the sunlight made us feel happy as the night was full of darkness and sadness. The natural radiance transformed us as the palace lit up in different shades of yellow and orange, which made us glad but also anxious—anxious to succeed and glad to have crossed the fatal night. Due to this transition, our eyes couldn't open as they were used to darkness, but it was so beautiful that they wanted to be open themselves! We were also acclamatised to a temperature in the night of zero degree Celsius, which was super cold, but as we entered the day, our bodies got goose bumps due to the change in temperature, and we felt like going to the beach after entering the day with temperature fifteen degree Celsius.

Another voice said, 'Hi folks. I am the boss here! Congratulations. You all have successfully crossed the nocturnal area, and I must say that you all here are indeed the lucky ones. I said "lucky ones", not winners, mind that. Lucky because you all are out alive from all the clues, and you will be glad to know that now, in my area, in the villain's area, there are no more clues. All you have to look out for is the key and the perfectly correct lock of statement. Mind you! I said no more clues, not "no more deaths"!'

CHAPTER 16

Next was Sminka's turn. A real faint heart, but she died when an arrow pierced her. It hit her right across her. A young girl, dying a cruel death, just in a flash, was the most unbearable sight for all of us. 'Not an end to the deaths.' I remembered what the 'villain' said. 'Not an end to cruel and pitiful deaths.' He should have said!

Facancia was uncontrollable. She said in a sad and disheartened tone, 'My sister, my brother, my twin, my mother, my father, my teacher, you were everything for me. I love you twin. Come back, please do.' We all held Facancia as we knew that Sminka was her only one left. Everybody in her family had died, and she couldn't bear the pain of Sminka's loss. I could understand her feelings—we all could. Losing the only one you have, the one closest and dearest to you, is not bearable for anybody, then how could a young girl like Facancia face it? I felt really sorry for her.

I couldn't be Sminka for Facancia, but I could definitely be a friend. 'Thanks, I don't need it', she said. But I wasn't offended. I could understand her pain as she was as emotional as me.

Instead of feeling sad for Sminka's death, we actually felt sorry for Facancia. There were tears in every person's eyes. Part two of the challenge didn't seem any better!

Facancia was trying to be brave, strong, courageous. Not like Sester. She knew she couldn't be like her. She understood pretty well that every second in there was precious and we had no time to waste. But understanding all this at this tender age, it made me fall in love with her instantly. I felt like giving her a tight hug, wanted to make her feel as warm as I could, to console her, to be there for her, but she didn't need any of it. That's the kind of girl I always wanted to be myself, and there she was, my Idol. I started feeling restless for this petite young girl, but she stood up strong and said, 'Let's proceed.'

That gave me a jerk. Someone whom you love the most isn't easy to forget, but Facancia learnt to move on in life. Yes, she did cry for a minute, but unlike Sester, she didn't waste an hour. She was so brave. Every hour, a new death just taught me a lesson. I was evolving with each death and experience, but this was so different, to learn a lesson so quickly from this beautiful young girl who has a very different mindset and from her sister who could do anything for her. I wished I could be a part of their family just to make a difference to her and replace her sister somehow.

We walked ahead and finally reached about our destination, but the destination moved further. We followed it, but smash! Someone from our team had eaten sand—hot, burning brown sand—and there was vomit all over the place. He was Weenfer. I was happy that he survived. He was puking incessantly. Eating sand in nervousness was quite normal. It was a response to stimulus for all that we were going through. Mixed emotions, anxiety for a 'closure', fed up of the slow moving time, fear of what's up next; it was not shocking at all for any of us that someone could eat sand; as, in the heat in the desert, you can see a mirage and that just seemed to be what may have happened to Weenfer. Although later we learnt that that guy was so famished and tired with the long, never ending day, witnessing so many deaths and out of his senses almost, that sand seemed like food to him, and he quickly gobbled up lots of it. It was a mirage. How it works? Your eyes see something, but the brain sees something else and tells the organs to use it the way the brain has seen it, and the eyes mean nothing at that time. Eventually, the brain is the ruler of our body, and every single part of the body functions the way the brain wants it to. That's exactly why my mom always says, 'It's all in the mind', when I say, 'I'm tired', and she wants me to do something or when I say, 'This is impossible. I can't do it', and she knows I can do it if I think that I can. I could relate to her thoughts everytime I was actually able to do all those things she induced me to do; thus, I was here, so strong and capable. *I owe it to you mom* was the instant thought in my mind at that moment.

Soon though, the thoughts wandered again. I was sure someone was dead now. I could feel the escalating thought in my mind, in my heart, everywhere in my body since I felt my heart beat faster.

CHAPTER 17

A huge log-like barrier with mixed tones was passing through, which was attempting and targeting to kill Facancia, but Kensia plunged in front of her, and the enormous log, weighing up to hundred kilograms killed Kensia. Her legs got cut off from her body, and her blood splashed all around the hall, and her beautiful stockings were torn due to the heavy metallic object. Right in front of our eyes, we see the legs leave the body—another frightful and pitiful scene. *What more is this challenge going to unveil? How much more strong do we have to be to reach and survive till the end?* I wondered.

Mamothimo removed his first-aid kit for the second time and inspected her body. He took out a crepe bandage from the kit, but due to extreme damage and blood loss, Kensia had to leave the earth at an early age of fourteen.

I was glad that Facancia survived, but at the same time, I pitied Kensia who was incredibly courageous and never gave up. Facancia was the bravest of the lot but uncontrollable this time and definitely felt worse than Sminka's death. Someone, Kensia, had given her own life than to let Facancia in the death knell, but all that was left from her attempt to save Facancia was her own dead body, which Facancia sobbed on. Everyone loses someone out here, but Facancia's pain was understood as she lost two very precious people out here simultaneously.

Facancia Flear, a beautiful and stunning girl, was also one of the top ten millionaires in Africa, who built her own business within a month, a factory that produced amazing and unique items. The USP of these items were that they were patented. That's what took her into the list of the top ten millionaires of Africa and made her extremely rich at twenty years of age. After the amazing achievement of making it to the list, she married Ryan who was twenty-one. For a few months, they had a super successful relationship until Facancia became pregnant and miscarried the baby. Her bad luck played truant when her marriage reached the gates of the most terrible thing anyone could think of—divorce. Their divorce reached completion just fifteen days before entering this deadly palace, so I personally think that this was most stressful and herculean for Facancia to accept the challenge thrown to her side!

After all that had happened to Facancia, Sminka was her only confidante and looked after everything she needed. We all could understand and feel the pain that Facancia felt, but she was devastated compared to anyone in the group because when Sminka died, Kensia told her that she has another support, which was Kensia herself. That was the one and only reason why Facancia was controllable the previous hour, but this time, none of us even dared to get into close vicinity of Facancia as she was a ball of anger and sorrow. I tried to console her as a friend, but her only reply was, 'Don't come near me, or you shall also die. Whoever will come close to me shall perish. I have no one on this earth.' How much ever we tried to console her, we were unable to penetrate through her psyche. We could understand her feelings and, therefore, were compassionate. As we walked a bit ahead, we saw a huge, transparent board with hooks. On the hooks were pinned up ninety-two keys which were enormously huge in size, and on each key was written a special word. 'You have to look out for the lock with the perfect key.' I remembered. The hour was almost over, but what we saw was that there was a one kilometer distance between each key, so we would definitely get exhausted. We were blank and didn't know which key to choose.

CHAPTER 18

The sun shone bright in the sky, and the weather was scorching hot. And to our sheer disbelief, we observed it come close and hit Trithpill like lightening would strike. We were standing close to Trithpill, but the power was affecting only Trithpill, and he started acting funny, with different structures and poses. He died in a minute due to direct heat filled in his body as he was sun burnt. His body was charred. We ran towards the first key, abandoning Trithpill's body. We tried lifting it to read the first word that was engraved on it, but it was so heavy that we needed at least four people to even move it. Then I applied logic and said, 'All the keys are placed in a horizontal position in such a manner that we can see only one side of it. If we have to move or invert each key, it's going to take us a lot of time, and we don't have time here. What we can do is go on the other side where the key is facing with the letters showing in that direction, and the board in the middle is transparent, so we can easily look at the words on each key without even touching them.' 'Brilliant', said a few voices together, and we all agreed to rush up to the other side except Facancia. She questioned, 'If we find the correct key, how would we take it to proceed towards the lock?' I was blank and dumbstruck as I didn't think of it and, thus, didn't have an answer to that. Tonthany and Mamothimo looked around and noticed that there was a semicircular hole at the bottom for us to reach towards the other side, and we could definitely take the way back to this side they explained. So we went towards the board area. The first key we read and saw had the word 'Lend' written on it, which probably meant 'offerings' to all discussed quickly. 'This is not what we are looking for', said Mamothimo. Without questioning him, or reasoning his statement, we all started running in a fast pace as we had to cover a long distance of one kilometer to reach the next key. We took fifteen minutes to get to the next one, and by then, we were completely drained. We read the next key, which said 'Sweet', and we just somehow knew that this was not the correct key, so we went towards the next key and took a lot more time to reach to it as we were tired and meek. When we reached it, the time was already 4.40 p.m. We read on the key 'Lendor', which meant fur (that was what Shakes thought), but we weren't convinced as we couldn't relate it anywhere. So we decided to open our 'Tech-Advance Information Device', and on opening it, we learnt that it meant money. Was money more important than lives to our king? We were puzzled. Suddenly, I remembered that the king once said, 'First health, and then wealth.' We were absolutely sure that Lendor wasn't the correct key, so we hurried to the next one. By the time we reached the next key, we had only five minutes in hand. We got nervous and scared. We quickly read the next key, which said 'Tick'. We discussed about it and were sure that the king would not send thirty-one young warriors to lose their lives just for a tick! While running in the direction of the next key, I remembered a saying said by my father, 'Feel death while you are alive. You should be scared of exiting this planet but not even so much that you can lose your existence. Don't be funny. Don't be a waste. Being funny in tough situations relaxes you, but it wastes a lot of time due to which it makes you useless! Work towards your destiny. Find some work. Work and learn much better. Death is poor. Death is weak. Death is sure but not so soon.

Death can happen in different ways that can make people feel poor and weak. Death is definitely going to occur, but being brave helps for death not now, not so soon. Don't lose hope till you are alive. Hope can stay when no one is with you. So till you are alive, let hope live with you.' I thought this was very much applicable in such a kind of a situation.

CHAPTER 19

The road started moving and split into two deep edged halves. I observed Tonthany falling and shouted his name aloud. Mamothimo got alert and held Tonthany's hand and tried pulling him up and edged off. There was deep water in there with dirty sand and blood. Tonthany was saved, but Mamothimo was in the hands of evil. The split built up and Mamothimo started sinking in. Soon his lungs were filled with water, and he seemed breathless. It was a very dirty sight, seeing the water, so one could imagine his predicament in there. He was not in the condition to walk, so he crawled up to me and said in his sinking but still bold voice, 'I appoint you as the next leader as you are my sister's daughter and undoubtedly the most capable.' 'Sister's daughter'—this new unknown fact was unacceptable and unbelievable for me. I fell towards the ground. I wondered how he was my uncle and what was the mystery behind the story, and why was it untold to me all these years. But it was not the appropriate time for analysis. Instead, I wanted to give my newly-found uncle a tight hug, but he was dead by then. This was a minute of sorrow and grief for the entire group, especially me, not only because he was my leader but also because he was my new-found uncle. Everybody knows how difficult it is to accept the death of an acquaintance, but I didn't know.

There was pain in every heart there, and they all surely felt very weak at that moment, not only for losing another group member or our leader but for the irreplaceable loss of the one and only person there who brought us comfort and made us feel positive about being able to see the end. The only hope, the only strength we all had was Mamothimo, and he was no more. I knew that I wouldn't prove to be a better leader than Mamothimo—nobody would! I knew that all of this was planned and just wished and hoped that had I known of the plan, I would attempt to save a life, probably Mamothimo's or Kensia's. Mamothimo meant a lot to the team. Nobody knew he was my uncle, not even me! But because of his last words 'I appoint you the next leader', everybody looked up to me as their new leader. I was blank. I wondered whether Mamothimo had planned my leadership or was it just a spontaneous decision? And if he planned, then did he know he was going to die? And how? At that moment, I started speaking loudly in the air, 'Mom, why didn't you tell me? I could have done something.' Everybody around pitied me, but they couldn't see their new leader in such a condition. It was a moment of remorse. Facancia too cried out loudly and said, 'Mamothimo was not only your uncle. He meant equally much to all of us.' Lonta started fidgeting with her ponytails, and she was sobbing discreetly. Tears dripped from everybody's eyes, and nobody was pacifiable, especially me. Tonthany blamed himself to be responsible for Mamothimo's death and said to me, 'You shouldn't have called out my name. You should have let me fall in there. At least our guide, our inspiration, our motivator would have been alive.' I had no words, no answer to that, as silently, deep within my heart, I kind of agreed with him and felt guilty but couldn't give him a consent. Midget had a lot of roses, which he placed near Mamothimo's body. We wanted to leave this palace, this unfriendly and cruel earth. I couldn't even vent out my tears as everybody looked up to me as their leader. I had no intention of becoming the leader, but I had no choice. Yes, I agree that every hour, every minute, every second was precious in this palace, but how could I not be upset at my uncle's death. It was impossible. I was on crossroads mentally. The clock was soon going to strike again, and all of us felt cheated by the ghost and the villain too. We all had come here for a fate, the fate-to-die, it felt at that moment. We knew that every hour someone will die—every hour! But we were still not prepared. We sniffed our noses and wiped our tears with the handkerchiefs provided by the king in our mini bag.

I gently and slowly picked up the communicating device and the other equipment the leader needed lying next to his cold body, feeling terrible and almost dead myself. Happy moments were relished as the time spent with our great leader was over, trying to overpower the sad feelings. I could proudly say, with all my confidence, that I was like his daughter, and I promised to myself that I will make him proud of me one day.

CHAPTER 20

Himlona Shrub was next to die. She somehow knew it, or maybe it was just an intuition. She said in a confident but low tone, 'War is on my side.' Before we could question her what that meant, a banana wrap took over her life. She slipped on a banana peel and fell straight down on her head, and it split into pieces, scattering blood all around. Dying by slipping on a banana peel was indeed very rare, and nobody could expect such a death in the palace. It was more obvious now that death was preplanned in the palace, and there was no escape route from it. The situation in the palace was getting very eerie. Everyone was petrified.

As I was holding the communicating device, I got a call on it, and I quickly answered it. The voice on the other end said, 'Congratulations! You are now the new leader. Sad to hear that Mamothimo died. He's your uncle.' I immediately understood that it was the owner of the palace, and he was calling just to waste our time. If he had an important message to say, he would have said it out aloud in the air as he did earlier, so my brains worked precisely, and I sensed it. I hung up instantly so as to not waste any more time.

Suddenly, the phone rang again, and I thought it's the same silly call. In an angry tone, I answered it, 'What is it? We are not interested in knowing whether you are sad or happy!' But it was not him this time. The hurried voice on the other end ordered, 'Give the phone to Mamothimo. Just tell me he is alive. I just want to hear that he is alive. Please tell me so because I can feel it that he is dead.' I replied in a sad tone, 'He is dead.' She began to cry incessantly as she always did. My voice was so low that it didn't register to her that it was me on the line, or maybe she didn't expect me to answer it, or even maybe she was so panicky that her sense organs weren't up to their best. She said, 'My brother is dead? Is he really dead? But Riya is OK, right? I can feel it. She is OK, right? Just tell me she is alright.' I could feel the love in her voice and the urgency of her need for me. I wanted to fall down in her lap at that very moment, but it was still time for it, so I had to console myself only with her voice. 'I'm Riya mom', I said. Happiness filled her body, and I could sense it in her voice now when she said, 'Riya, my love, you are fine darling. I'm waiting, come soon. I'm so proud of you my baby.' And I asked her, 'If he is your brother, why didn't you ever divulge it to me?' She replied, 'I always knew that I had another brother named Mamo, but my parents told me that he was lost, and they thought that he was dead. The day when the names were announced he came up to me and revealed that he was my long lost brother and that he had changed his name to Mamothimo. I was panic-stricken too but also delighted and emotional to find my brother. He didn't want me to reveal this to you. He also told me that he has five daughters, one of which was kidnapped when she was two months old.' I told her, 'Mom, you don't know how I felt! It was shocking! A lost uncle suddenly appearing from nowhere!' Mom apologized profusely and said that she had to because she was bound by her long lost brother's promise, and the line got disconnected. I was so glad that she called. Her voice, her excitement on knowing I'm alive, her feeling proud of me, all these just gave me a kick, and I felt as fresh as I had started. I felt energised. My tempo was back, and once again, I was charged with my positive outlook. My happiness knew no bounds at that moment, just by listening to my mum's voice! I couldn't imagine how she must have managed to get hold of the number which to call on, as there was no access and also a very big secret. But then I thought, *Moms are moms. They can do anything,* and smiled to myself at that thought.

CHAPTER 21

The clock struck and Shakes was invisible. He disappeared in a fraction of a second. Then with a torn and pierced body, he returned, and in front of our eyes, he collapsed and died! None of us knew how he died or where he had gone, but we were sure that the evil incarnate was responsible. Lee Whatlever was stunned that his wife's brother, a benevolent person like Shakes Alora, had left the world. His pictures of kindness flashed before our eyes. Lonta and Shakes were good friends, and that obviously concluded that Lonta felt sad. It was amazing that there was nobody in the palace who didn't have a connection or a close knit person and so did Lonta. Shakes and Lonta were inseperable. Infinities meant less here. Everyone had a memory or something to remember about whoever was lost there! Shakes always tried to help others, and his attempt was more than anyone could expect. His death made all of us upset, but we just didn't have the power and courage to lose another hour, another life, and another teammate. I must mention that Shakes was hardly visible. His body was torn into bits and pieces. We decided to move ahead, avoiding the disheartening sight of his dead body.

We had to travel another kilometer to reach the next key, which ultimately we did! On it was written, 'Life'. 'That's it! Done! We found the key. The key for statement is life!' I shouted in excitement and sheer joy. I was sure, very sure, and absolutely convinced that this was the key because it made total sense, and also I was in control of my gut feeling, which had never let me down. We all lit up with joy. What was unimaginable was that it was just the fifth key out of so many, and we found the correct one so soon. That's means that the bad man actually wanted us to get to the statement. We felt proud and protected that fate was drawing close, fate was not death, and now, soon we would reach the end alive! We all felt an adrenaline rush and an elated feeling of being on top of the world—jubilant to the core.

All of us formed a queue, intending to reach the other side, as the keys and locks were there, and we had come on this side to just see the reflected parts of the keys in order to read what was written on them. I was first to crawl through, and it wasn't hard for a skinny body like mine. Next was Facancia. She too slipped in easily. It was not difficult for the others too except for Tencia, for she was plump and, thus, was unable to come out. We all tried hard, and with no success to do so, we had to finally break the glass with hammers and other heavy objects lying around. It took quite long to get her through. Tencia felt dejected as she realized that she wasted a lot of time, but she was also a part of the team, so how could we let go of her?

We rushed towards the key. I held the rear part of the key, Ella held the front, Tonthany held the centre part, and all of us proceeded. Not far away, a small door appeared, which opened automatically as we got close. What we saw next was a maze where we had to search for the appropriate lock. There were several locks, out of which finding the correct one seemed like another task. Not to be mentioned here, one can imagine that if the key was so huge, how big would the lock be?!

CHAPTER 22

The time had come once again! Tonthany wanted to look at the time, so he had to turn his wrist. As a result, the grip through our fingers got loose, and the key slipped from our hands! Obviously, the weight of the key was too much, and it manifested. Tencia died due to the weight of the key on her body. It was also about to smack Lonta too, but Fonsenca leaped and moved Lonta. This action of hers saved Lonta but killed Fonsenca herself. Lonta's eyes were numb; her heart was torn. She started to wail. I grabbed her in my arms and wiped her tears. She hugged me tight as she couldn't bear the pain of losing her sister at such a tender age. I knew I shouldn't let go of the warmth I was giving her, so I asked Facancia if she would hold the key. Of course, she didn't mind it, as she knew the pain of losing a sister. Holding Lonta tight, we continued moving ahead.

We tried the key in two locks but in vain. It didn't fit in either. Now I started doubting if the key was correct! I couldn't show my apprehension to the other team members, as I wasn't sure myself, and also that I didn't want them to panic. There was no time for it. By now, with the tension and the weight of the key and all the running around, we were extremely tired and desperately hungry. We kept the key down and decided to take a five minute break from our precious time. Time was definitely running out, but with no energy to move, the break was important. All of us removed our tablets and filled up our craving stomachs. After we ate our tablets, we were imagining scrumptious flavours of Coke and burgers. Tablets are not a good idea for people on an important mission where they do need energy. It was unsatisfactory to our minds. Eating food is a mind game, which we feed our brain and energise ourselves and not just fill ourselves up. This was not enough for us. Eating an item and then having a drink on it is better than anything. This seemed inappropriate.

Every minute, I was more and more depressed because as a leader, I was ineffective in helping my teammates. Failure is what I felt because my teammates' number and chances to win were depleting. I wanted to help people who were dying every hour, wanted to save each and every person who was still alive, and wanted to reach our destination soon, but when I was helpless myself, how could I assist anybody else! I felt useless and worthless!

CHAPTER 23

Stupidity doesn't stop following certain people. It is a behavior that shows a lack of good sense or judgment, dumbness, foolishness, brainlessness, ignorance, mindlessness, dull-wittedness, doltishness, slowness, vacancy, etc., and this is exactly what struck Wentor. In order to endeavour to pick a lock, he passed away. We wondered what he was thinking. Such fool hardiness! He got crushed under the weight of the mammoth lock. What a waste of a life! It intrigued me, and I wanted to talk a lot about stupidity and its reasons, as we had previously learnt about it. But then I thought that I couldn't waste time like that as we had a lot of labour to do in order to reach our destination.

We checked about fifteen locks that hour, but none of them were accurate. The feeling that maybe the key is not the correct one, maybe we hurried too much on making ourselves sure that this was the correct one led to nervousness and panic within me. We could feel the fear rise up our nerves; it was killing us. Fear keeps us focused on the past or keeps us worried about the future. If we can overcome our fear, we can realize that right now we are okay. Right now, today, we are still alive, and our bodies and our brains are still working marvelously. Our eyes can still see the beautiful sky and our ears can still hear the voices of our loved ones. What's important is to understand and accept at that moment is that thinking will not overcome fear but action will. The oldest and strongest fear of mankind is fear, and the oldest and the strongest fear is fear of the unknown—fear of uncertainty. When actually the only thing we really have to fear is fear itself. What is fear of living? It is being pre-eminently afraid of dying. That is not what you came here to do, out of timidity and spinelessness. The antidote is to take full responsibility for yourself, for the time you take up, and for the space you occupy. If you don't know what you are here for, then just do some good. There is no passion as contagious as that of fear. It is similar to catching an express train and definitely one will emerge victorious.

Carrying the key was not as easy as anyone would think it to be. If so much weight and pressure is on you, then you definitely get tired. Depression, which comes when you are sad and makes you sadder, can also make you feel drained of energy. It can stop you from getting sleep.

We had a fate to do all this, beholding death, hour by hour. Water—was it more important than so many lives? Will power was the only thing that motivated us to charge ahead. It is positive approach that guided us. Time was striking each hour! Each minute increased my heart beat, and each second, I was putting myself down as the leader. I wanted to save everybody's lives. I am ordinary but ready to become special. The team was already too depressed to lose another leader. I felt I should hand over the team to Facancia and die. No point in living when you are lifeless, witnessing so much bloodshed and fatality. Bearing so many deaths isn't easy. But at the same time, I didn't want to break Mamothimo's trust.

Something abominable was occurring in my house, in my town. I could sense it. I could feel the sadness escalating till my heart, and

I was so desperate to know what. Something was not right for my family—an occurrence that sent shivers. Something had definitely happened. My heart screeched out a very gloomy thought, but I failed. My tears were in my heart, not on my face. Insecurity of loved ones, tension of their well being, worry, fear—maybe all these come into you when you are ready to die! A premonition, was it?

Another thought I was getting was that maybe the scoundrel planned his actions that the ones to die in such a manner would be the intelligent, helpful, and fully-dedicated people. That scared me more, as even I was one of them. I wanted to return home, see my parents, hug them, and see them being proud of me. I wanted to return to them safe and sound. I panicked, but what could have been done! Absolutely nothing! The team was tired and so was I.

CHAPTER 24

A little further ahead, we thought we saw an illusion of a female poodle, which was a middle sized female dog. She was as white as snow and had a beautiful red bow against her head. She was furry and hairy on her ears, legs, and tail. Ella's pet, Bratty, saw this beautiful female and seemed attracted. She was gorgeously sweet, and it was evident that Bratty couldn't resist going close to her. As soon as he approached her, she receded. He pursued for about five minutes but couldn't. Ella touched it, trying to grab Bratty, and as soon as she did that, what seemed like an illusionary poodle turned into a real poisonous one and bit Ella on her hand. Bratty barked out loud and felt betrayed. Ella was his owner since he was a new born puppy, and she was his mother. I felt very sorry for him. Lonta patted his fur to make him feel better. Facancia held him tight and didn't let go until he didn't stop crying, but tears in his eyes didn't stop till the end. We could sense the poor dog's sentiments. Ella died an unexpected death.

What Hanah noticed was unnoticeable among so many of us. All the locks were huge, but the most mammoth of them was number thirty-two, and she said immediately, pointing out at it, 'I personally think it is this one, as it seems like the biggest one.' I replied, 'If we have tried so many, what is the harm with one more. Let's do it. Hopefully, your intuition might be correct.' Immediately, the wrongdoer cried in the background. 'No! It's not that one. Don't make me fierce enough to kill all of you. You are not opening that one. That's an order! Or else, the result will not be in your favor.'

He thought that his words would affect us, but we didn't even bother to care about his malicious orders. He was just trying to distract us and why not? He would have to give away Instatusquo! This was just one of his tactics to stop us from reaching our destiny. But we decided to listen to our instincts. Our fate was lying right there in front of us, and nothing or nobody could over power us to reach to it. Our destiny makers would make sure that the warning given by him would have to lead to something hazardous—we all knew it. And they also tried to take away Bratty from us as they knew he would give way to the lock. He kept barking ferociously near lock number thirty-two, but we didn't notice. They were unable to control Bratty's mind as humans have a different brain from dogs, and they knew he would give away, but fortunately, they couldn't take him away. With that note, we plunged forward to target number thirty-two as now we were sure that that was the one we were looking for. The lucky one! And our lucky Bratty!

CHAPTER 25

At that move, the evil architect wanted to actually kill every one of us, not giving the statement, and so he did attempt. A two-feet, long, twistable arrow shot Lenrica first, twisted towards the left and killed Weenfer, twisted right and hit Lee, twisted northeast and popped into Waliom, and then finally went straight and hit Hanah. She was the last one, and before giving away her last breath, she cried, 'Yes! I'm dead. You all shall succeed as I was the last one to die. Thank you God!' She indeed lived beautifully and died a heroic death. The destination we search for also searches us. It was a major loss for us to handle, but we were the victors of our mission—Facancia Fear, Tonthany Brusoe, Lonta Ambrace, Midget Kill, Bratty Phoes, Lomus Freelter, and me, Riya Mathews. We were the lucky ones, the ones alive yet.

I was feeling so proud to succeed with my six other friends, but at the same time high regards, condolences, and sorrow for my other twenty-three friends who all taught me a lot before leaving my side.

Heath- she barely entered the Palace and lost her life. She didn't witness the feel of the competition, I feel sorry for her.

Fleenker- She taught the entire team to not lose hope and not give up whatsoever the circumstances might be. A true fighter!

Demoler- Sester wasted an entire hour when Demoler died. Speaks volumes about his popularity.

Tases- Time is important is what I learnt from his death.

Flinco- 'Don't be over confident' is what I imbibed from Flinco.

Trinka- 'Be brave to face your own death.'

Trientika- I will never forget her for saving my life. What a close brush with death!

Sester- Her circumstances resulted in harm to her child. I emphathised with her.

Sminka- 'Always learn to be generous to your family and then others' was her mantra.

Kensia- 'Help people who do need your support' was her philosophy.

Trithphill- 'Be helpful and people will never forget you' is what he believed in.

Mamothimo- Being a good leader, he was a good person too I strongly feel.

Himlona- To always control your body and be cautious at all times.

Shakes- Taught me to be careful and lovable.

Tencia- Lived to make people happy, and that feeling was refreshing.

Fonsenca- 'Love your family and do anything to save them', she always said.

Wentor- 'Do not be stupid' was his mind.

Ella- 'Prove yourself till the last day'—what a conviction.

My tributes to Lenrica, Weenter, Lee, and Waliom.

Hanah- Help, support, and be the hero.

Death was close to everyone. Death is poor, death is weak, death is certain but not so soon. At that moment, I remembered my promise to my father that I wouldn't lose hope. Then why should I! If you promise to be alive till your hundredth, so be it. All I want to say is that whenever you are in such a situation, don't lose heart. Face it. Prove yourself; take it positively rather than feeling depressed about it. If you think positively, you can think rationally and become a victor just like Facancia or Lonta, whereas a negative mind frame could bring death to you like Sester's. I know that my story doesn't convey that to the fullest because people like Mamothimo, Fonsenca, and Hanah had to face death despite being strong and positive. Start new, start better, and don't ever give up.

CHAPTER 26

Hearts filled with gratitude and humbleness, we inserted the 'Life' key in the largest lock and turned it anti-clockwise. It unlocked instantly, and our faces lit up with joy. There was no end to our happiness, but at the same time, we were curious to read out the statement. There was a sudden change in the atmosphere. All the disturbing sounds in the air, the rustling of things unseen stopped, the sights of fearful objects disappeared, and the air became pure and clean as though showering us with love. Everything was purely magical, divine, and beautiful.

Being the Leader, I took authority to remove the nicely folded, well decorated, and amazingly powerful chart and unfolded it.

LIFE DOESN'T LIE BENEATH THE FEET OF GOD.

This is the statement that snuffed away twenty-three precious lives but will save thousands of lives and will give respite to many, but I was hoping to understand it totally.

But, thankfully, another announcement in the air, in a soft, sweet, polite, and explaining voice spoke:

'God doesn't control your life. It is you who control it yourself.

Life doesn't lie beneath the feet of God.

This is your life-saver Statement. Every citizen whose last words are these will live to see his hundredth. That is why the king sent so many of you. Many died, but many will live long because of those dead, because of their sacrifice.

Now let me explain the statement to you all.

Every day, we take our own decisions. God doesn't come to us to tell us what to do. He only sends different waves to us at varied phases of life. These waves are in the form of thoughts, actions, power, ideas, likes, and dislikes. Which wave to surf is entirely up to us, and each one of us does that on our own.

Beliefs and emotions towards prayers are important. But remember that if you want your prayers to be answered and your wishes to be fulfilled, make sure your deeds are worth them. As good will get good, and evil will be given evil.

So folks, instead of leaving everything on God and blaming things on Him or on destiny, remember that you have to take responsibility of your deeds, and, thus, you have to make sure your actions and thoughts are always the way you want it back, for the golden rule of life is, 'Treat others the way you want to be treated', 'Think the way you want to be remembered', and keeping this in mind, be successful in overpowering the wrong waves.

Last but not the least, 'God helps those who helps themselves.' This saying was prominent and evident years ago, but with time, people have forgotten it. It's time to believe in it again.

Good luck to you all. Congratulations once again and all the best to you for taking charge of your life. Happy living!'

CHAPTER 27

A lesson well learnt! And totally worth it! With content hearts, bidding a final goodbye to our fellow mates, who had sacrificed their lives for a better future of the town, we proceeded towards the exit.

It took us twenty-seven minutes to reach to the exit point, where the cars were waiting for us through the day. The same day which seemed like ages, now felt like just a few hours. We were both anxious and excited to meet our near and dear ones. I couldn't wait for a single more moment to meet my family.

Everybody outside was waiting to welcome us. As we stepped out of the gate, bright sunlight and fresh air welcomed us. Families of all the thirty-one who went in were eagerly awaiting us. There was loud cheering and clapping as soon as we were seen. It felt like we were superstars, heroes for all of them.

For the people who did not see their family members, it was a time of depression and remorse. Many cried out aloud, some didn't react, while some I think had already accepted it and, thus, clapped and cheered for the ones who made it.

A single day, just twenty-four hours, had transformed my life from an ordinary citizen to a hero. People lifted me up and gave me immense importance on knowing that I was the leader, guiding, helping, and taking decisions for my team. My eyes were still searching for my parents as they were elusive. After about nine or ten minutes, I saw my parents running towards me from a distant end. We ran towards each other, and as soon as I neared them, I leaped and fell into my mom's arms. My dad opened out his arms too around us, and we had the warmest family hug ever! One by one, we all kissed each other endlessly. I could feel the tears on my cheeks and hands—tears of happiness! None of us had anything to say. Ecstasy out of something unexpected and the feeling of being alive and back after witnessing traumatic experiences at close quarters were incomprehensible to me and my family.

All the victors started bidding goodbyes with thank you notes and gratitude. Everybody was joyous. Contentment shone in their sparkling eyes. There were smiles on every face. Just as about almost all had left, Facancia came up to me and gave me a tight hug. She had a 'no look' face, and I noticed, for some reason, her eyes didn't want to meet mine. I told her, 'I'm sorry for you, Facancia. Do let me know if there's anything I can do for you.' She kept quiet, avoiding eye contact. I was sure something was troubling her. I asked, 'Do you want to confide in me? Say it please.' She looked at my mom and then at me, again at my mom, again at me, and in a hesitant voice, she said, 'Mr Mamothimo is no more! He is dead! I lived my entire life as an orphan along with my sister. Only after losing my father, I got to know that he was my father. Mamothimo left me a note, which he secretly handed over to me while dying. I learnt that he was my father. He couldn't tell it to me when he was alive, but he didn't want to leave the world with such a big secret in his heart.'

I was awestruck. 'I am also here to lose something.' I remembered Mamothimo's words. I looked at my mom. She knew it all. She too avoided eye contact with me and gave Facancia a hug. I felt really sorry for her because having a father alive and still having to live an orphan's life must be traumatic. I could empathise with her.

After feeling a bit better with my mom's hug, Facancia said, 'Dad has also mentioned in the letter about how I am related to you. He has requested to you and your family that he no longer wants me to live a lonely life. I have relatives, a family in this town itself, and that is only you all. Can you please fulfill my father's last wish and accept me as a part your family so that I can live with my own people?'

My mom and I said in monotone, 'Of course, you can. And you have to live with us only, now and forever.' We all hugged each other and welcomed our new family member, Facancia. We were all ecstatic. Facancia too was overwhelmed. She had tears in her eyes. Her newly found family felt like a blessing to her, and she was highly thankful to us for it. I got an elder sister. I was very happy about that too.

From a pauper, whose family had trouble making ends meet, we transformed into a family who was one of the top ten millionaires with a lifelong supply of 'precious water'. Courage and will power, positive outlook and belief, good actions, good thoughts, and fearlessness rewarded me with everything I could ask for. I was a hero, and I was proud of myself, as much as my family was.

This is my new life, a superstar life, giving speeches and interviews everywhere on all news channels, in all papers, magazines—everything with big banners and hoardings of mine all around the world, having belief in God and in myself.

My story has just now begun.